M m

Muhammad's Monday and the Letter **M**

Alphabet Friends

by Cynthia Klingel and Robert B. Noyed

The Child's World

**Published in the United States of America
by The Child's World®**
P.O. Box 326
Chanhassen, MN 55317-0326
800-599-READ
www.childsworld.com

The Child's World®: Mary Berendes, Publishing Director

Editorial Directions, Inc.: E. Russell Primm, Editorial
Director; Emily Dolbear, Line Editor; Ruth Martin,
Editorial Assistant; Linda S. Koutris, Photo Researcher
and Selector

Photographs ©: AFP/Corbis: Cover & 9; James P. Blair/
Photodisc/Getty Images: 10; Corbis: 13, 17, 18;
Rubberball Productions/Getty Images: 14; Michael
Matisse/Photodisc/Getty Images: 21.

Library of Congress Cataloging-in-Publication Data
Klingel, Cynthia Fitterer.
  Muhammad's Monday and the letter M / by Cynthia
Klingel and Robert B. Noyed.
    p. cm. — (Alphabet readers)
Summary: A simple story about how a boy named
Muhammad and his mother spend their Monday
introduces the letter "m".
  ISBN 1-59296-103-7 (Library Bound : alk. paper)
  [1. Mothers and sons—Fiction. 2. Alphabet.] I. Noyed,
Robert B. II. Title. III. Series.
  PZ7.K6798Mu 2003
  [E]—dc21   2003006606

Note to parents and educators:
The first skill children acquire before becoming successful readers is individual letter recognition. The Alphabet Friends series has been created with the needs of young learners in mind. Each engaging book begins by showing the difference between the capital letter and the lowercase letter. In each of the books on the vowels and the consonants c and g, children are introduced to the different sounds that the letter can make. Finally, children see that the letters can be found at the beginning of a word, in the middle of a word, and in most cases, at the end of a word.

Following the introduction, children meet their Alphabet Friends. The friend in each story encounters many words that include the featured letter of that book. Each noun that begins with the title letter is highlighted in red with the initial letter of the word in bold. Above the word is a rebus drawing that establishes a strong picture cue.

At the end of each book, we have included three words lists. Can your young learners find all the words in each book with the title letter in them?

Let's learn about the letter **M.**

The letter **M** can look like this: **M.**

The letter **M** can also look like this: **m.**

The letter **m** can be at the beginning of a word, like milk.

milk

The letter **m** can be in the middle of a word, like animals.

ani**m**als

The letter **m** can be at the

end of a word, like room.

roo**m**

It is a special **M**onday.  **M**uhammad and

his **m**other will do many things.

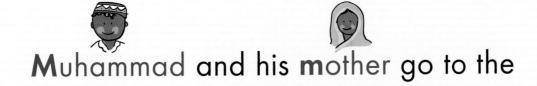

Muhammad and his mother go to the

mailbox. They have many letters to

mail to family and friends. Muhammad

drops the letters in the mailbox.

It's time for the **m**ovie! At the **m**ovie,

 Muhammad sees his friend **M**aggie.

"Maybe you can sit next to me!"

says **M**uhammad.

The **m**ovie is over. **M**uhammad waves

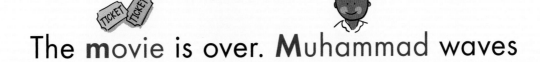

goodbye to **M**aggie. **M**uhammad and

his **m**other have many more things to do.

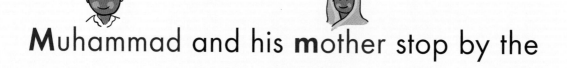

Muhammad and his mother stop by the

supergmarket. Muhammad finds macaroni

to make for dinner. They also buy milk.

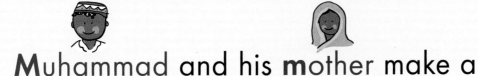 Muhammad and his mother make a

 snack. Muhammad likes to munch on

  cookies and drink milk. "More milk!"

says Muhammad.

It has been a marvelous **M**onday.

Muhammad and his **m**other did many

things. There is more to do tomorrow.

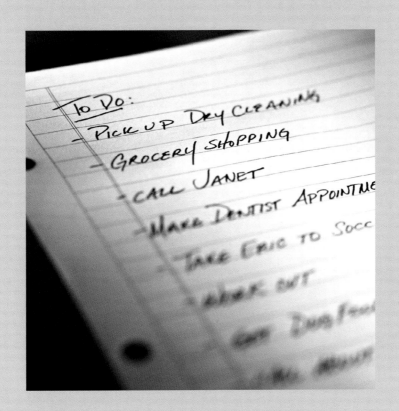

Fun Facts

Do you want to mail a letter to someone? You can take it to a post office, or drop it in a **m**ailbox. A **m**ailbox is a place where letters are put so that they can be picked up by a mail carrier. If you live in a city or large town, there might be **m**ailboxes along many of the streets. Mail carriers take the letters and packages from the **m**ailboxes to a nearby post office where the mail is sorted. Then your letter can finally be delivered!

Do you like to watch **m**ovies? Nowadays, watching **m**ovies is a very popular way to have fun. But **m**ovies are a fairly new invention. If you lived more than 100 years ago, you might never have seen one. The first real motion picture was shown in 1895. **M**ovies were called *motion* or *moving pictures* back then. They were also a lot different than the **m**ovies we watch in theaters and at home today. Until the 1920s, motion pictures were usually silent, black and white, and very short.

To Read More

About the Letter M

Klingel, Cynthia, and Ballard, Peg. *Malls: The Sound of M*. Chanhassen, Minn.: The Child's World, 2000.

About Mailboxes

Fremont, Eleanor, and Tom Leigh (illustrator). *A Surprise in the Mailbox*. New York: Simon Spotlight, 1999.

Poydar, Nancy. *Mailbox Magic*. New York: Holiday House, 2000.

Zoehfeld, Kathleen Weidner, and Mike Peterkin (illustrator). *Pooh's Mailbox*. New York: Disney Press, 1997.

About Movies

Avi, and C. B. Mordan (illustrator). *Silent Movie*. New York: An Anne Schwartz Book/Atheneum Books for Young Readers, 2002.

Numeroff, Laura Joffe, and Felicia Bond (illustrator). *If You Take a Mouse to the Movies*. New York: HarperCollins, 2000.

Rey, Margret A., and H. A. Rey (illustrator). *Curious George Goes to a Movie*. Boston: Houghton Mifflin Company, 1998.

Words with M

Words with **M** at the Beginning

macaroni

Maggie

mail

mailbox

make

many

marvelous

maybe

me

middle

milk

monday

more

mother

movie

Muhammad

munch

Words with **M** in the Middle

animals

family

Muhammad

supermarket

time

tomorrow

Words with **M** at the End

room

About the Authors

Cynthia Klingel has worked as a high school English teacher and an elementary teacher. She is currently the curriculum director for a Minnesota school district. Cynthia Klingel lives with her family in Mankato, Minnesota.

Robert B. Noyed started his career as a newspaper reporter. Since then, he has worked in communications and public relations for a Minnesota school district for more than fourteen years. Robert B. Noyed lives with his family in Brooklyn Center, Minnesota.